For Calum and Lorraine

First published in Great Britain and the USA in 2008 by
Frances Lincoln Children's Books, 4 Torriano Mews,
Torriano Avenue, London NW5 2RZ
www.franceslincoln.com

British Library Cataloguing in Publication Data available on request

ISBN: 978-1-84507-805-8

Set in Galliard and Truesdell

Printed in China

1 3 5 7 9 8 6 4 2

The
Land of the
Dragon King

and other Korean stories

Gillian McClure

F

FRANCES LINCOLN
CHILDREN'S BOOKS

Stories without feet travel far, if told.

Korean proverb

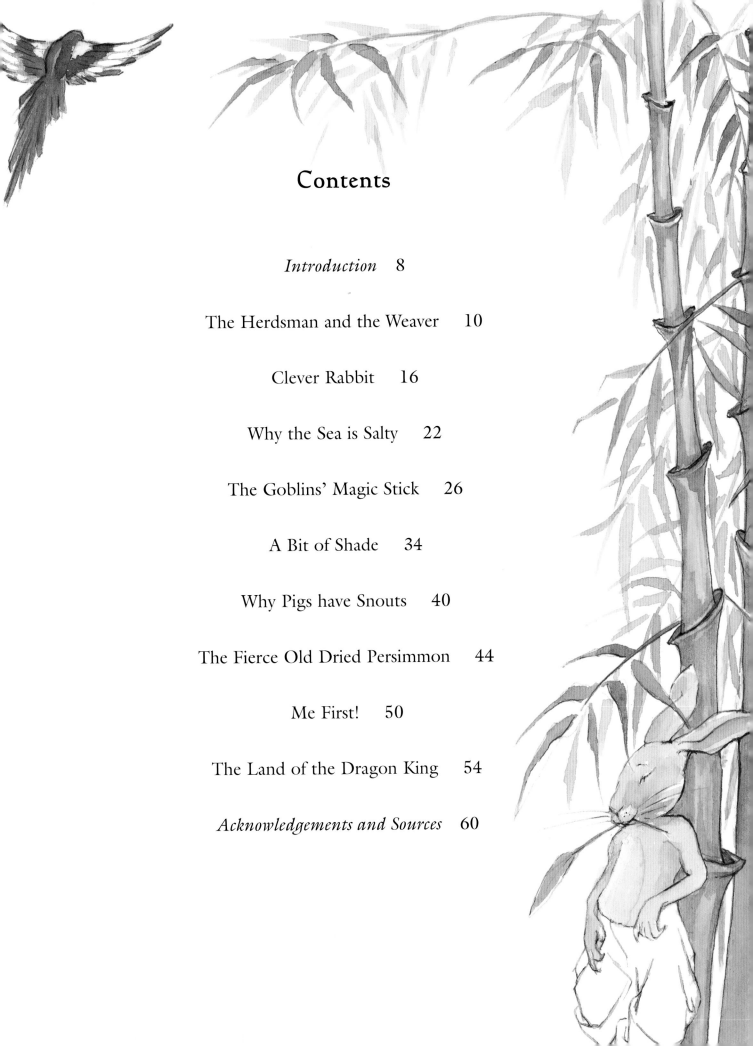

Contents

Introduction

I first visited South Korea in the 1990s to see my son, who was working with a shipping company in Ulsan. At that time there weren't many Europeans visiting South Korea. On my first day, I took a bus to Pusan. Once the bus left Ulsan with its high-rise flats, I caught a glimpse of villages, rice fields and the hills beyond. It was a landscape I recognised from the Korean folk tales I was reading, and I wanted to see more. The next day I hired a car and headed north. Up in the hills I found what I was looking for: traditional houses, some with blue roofs, a boy up a persimmon tree picking fruit, old women working in the rice fields, and grassy burial mounds deep in the woods.

Every day I went further into the hills. Once I got hopelessly lost, and only found my way back thanks to a kind taxi driver who wouldn't accept payment from me.

Before I left, I met up with a Korean editor and showed her my sketches. She encouraged me to illustrate this collection because, she told me, she wanted me to help Korean children 'hope and dream'. I hope that these stories will introduce children everywhere to Korea and bring them enchanting dreams from *The Land of the Dragon King*.

Gillian McClure

The Herdsman and the Weaver

There is a Land Beyond the Stars. And in the Land Beyond the Stars lives the Heavenly Ruler.

The Heavenly Ruler had a daughter who was a skilled weaver. Throughout her childhood she sat at her loom with the shuttle flying between the threads, weaving fine cloth. The Ruler was proud of his daughter's skill and when she grew up, he said, "My daughter must marry a man who is also skilled and hard-working."

After a long search, he found a prince from a neighbouring land who loved herding cows.

"The perfect match!" said the Ruler. "A prince and a princess, a herdsman and a weaver." And a royal wedding took place.

To begin with, all went well. The young couple worked hard at their herding and weaving. But as their love grew, all they wanted to do was to be with each other and play in the meadow.

Word soon reached the Heavenly Ruler that his daughter's loom was gathering dust and his son-in-law's cows had been left to roam. There was no fine cloth, and cows were trampling the palace gardens.

The Ruler grew angry. He decided that the young couple would have to live apart.

"You shall live in the West," he said to his daughter, "and go back to weaving fine cloth. "And you," he said to his son-in-law, "shall live in the East and go back to herding cows."

The young people were utterly miserable. Never had the Ruler seen two people look so sad.

He softened a little.

"You may meet once a year," he told them, "on the seventh day of the seventh moon, at the great river of the Milky Way."

So the weaver took her loom and went to live beyond the stars in the West, and the herdsman took his cows and went to live beyond the stars in the East. But their hearts were not in their work. They longed for the seventh day of the seventh moon, when they could be together.

At last the day came, and the lovers hurried to the banks of the Milky Way. As they waded across the great starry river, they reached out to one another. But their hands never touched. The Milky Way was too wide and too deep, and they were forced to turn back. Their tears flowed as they parted, the weaver returning to the West, and the herdsman to the East.

Meanwhile, on Earth it rained. For a whole year it rained. The animals were flooded out of their holes and burrows. They stared gloomily at the skies.

"Something must be causing all this rain," growled Bear.

"It's the herdsman and the weaver again," said Rabbit. "While they're apart, they will always weep, and down here it will always be raining."

"Then they must meet," said Bear.

"They tried, last year, on the seventh day
of the seventh moon," said Rabbit, "but the
Milky Way was too wide and deep to cross."
"They need a bridge," said Bear.
"Who will build them a bridge?"
Magpie said, "I'll build
them a bridge."
He flew off to
find all the other
magpies. Soon a
great flock had
gathered.

Then the magpies began their long flight up to the Milky Way and when they reached the great starry river, they hovered above it. With wing overlapping wing, and tail overlapping tail, they formed themselves into a bridge.

* * *

It was the seventh day of the seventh moon. The herdsman and the weaver hurried once more to the banks of the Milky Way. When they saw the magpie bridge they were overjoyed. They stepped lightly on to it and ran until they met in the middle. There they were in each other's arms, together at last.

Too soon, time ran out and the lovers were forced to part. They looked back and saw the magpie bridge break up as the birds flew away. But this time, when the weaver returned to the West and the herdsman to the East, fewer tears were shed.

Down on Earth, the rain turned to drizzle, then stopped. And every year since then, when the magpies build their bridge for the herdsman and the weaver, a few raindrops fall from the sky and you can see the lovers' two stars, Altair and Vega, shining brightly on either side of the Milky Way.

Clever Rabbit

A man was travelling over a wild mountain pass, when he heard a strange sound. It came from a deep, man-made pit.

The man paused. He peered down into the pit. At the bottom, looking up at him, was a tiger.

"Help! Help me out of here!" cried the tiger.

The man felt sorry for the creature – but he was also frightened.

"I'd like to help you," he said, "but you're a tiger and I'm a man. Tigers eat men."

"Tigers don't eat men who save them," moaned the tiger.

"If I get you out, will you promise not to eat me?" asked the man.

The tiger promised.

So the man let a branch down and pulled the animal out.

The tiger paced hungrily around the man.

"Stop that!" cried the man. "Remember, I rescued you."

"It was a man-made pit," growled the tiger. "So I've changed my mind. I'm going to eat you." And he edged closer, licking his lips with his long, wet tongue.

"Wait!" cried the man. "This isn't fair. Ask that pine tree over there. I'm sure it will agree."

The pine tree bent over to listen to the tiger's story. Then it straightened its trunk and rattled its twigs.

"Fair enough," it said. "Men destroy trees. They chop us into logs and burn us. Men deserve to be eaten."

"Then that's what I'll do," growled the tiger, and the man felt the beast's hot, hungry breath on his cheek.

"Wait!" cried the man. "This isn't fair. Ask that ox over there. I'm sure he will agree."

The ox raised his head and listened to the story. Then he swished his tail and snorted.

"Fair enough," he said. "All our lives we oxen work hard for men. We pull their ploughs and carry their loads. Then, when we're too old

to work, they slaughter us. I see nothing wrong in a tiger eating a man."

"Then that's what I'll do," growled the tiger, and the man heard two rows of sharp teeth grinding together.

"Wait!" cried the man. "Ask that rabbit over there to be the judge. If he agrees with the others, then you can eat me!"

The rabbit smiled as he listened to the story.

"I never believe anything men say," said the rabbit. "Show me that this pit really exists." So they led the rabbit to the pit.

"I still don't believe it," said the rabbit. "Show me what really happened." So the tiger showed the rabbit how he fell into the pit and then couldn't get out again.

The rabbit looked down at the tiger and thought for a moment. Then he said to the man, "Everything was fine until you helped the tiger out. So, to put things right, we should leave everything just as it was in the first place."

"You mean, leave the tiger in the pit?" asked the man.

"That's what I think," said the rabbit.

So that's how they left it.

The rabbit said goodbye,

      the man went on his way,

            ... and they left the tiger sitting down in the pit...

(but he managed to climb out later, when no one was looking).

Why the Sea is Salty

The sea hasn't always been salty. It took a thief to make it that way.

There once was a king who owned a hand-mill. It looked like any other small, stone hand-mill. But this was a magic hand-mill, and it could grind out whatever anyone asked for. If the king wanted gold, he just had to say: "I want gold. Grind, magic hand-mill, grind!" Then its handle would start to turn and gold would pour out, until the king said: "Stop, magic hand-mill, stop!"

A thief heard about the magic hand-mill, and one dark night he crept into the palace and stole it. Then, fearing that the king's horsemen would follow him, he stole a boat and rowed far out to sea.

Sitting in the boat, he looked at the hand-mill and wondered what to ask for. Not gold. People would talk and the king would hear of it. No, he would ask for something ordinary, something everyone wanted, something he could sell for a good price.

Salt! Everyone needs salt!

Quickly he said to the magic hand-mill, "I want salt. Grind, magic hand-mill, grind!" Even before he had finished saying the words, the handle started to turn and salt poured into the bottom of the boat.

The thief couldn't believe his eyes. He lifted up a handful. He was going to be rich! He started to sing and dance.

"Grind, magic hand-mill, grind!" he sang. "With the money from this salt I'll buy myself new clothes!"

The hand-mill went on grinding until the boat was full of salt, and still the thief sang, "Grind, magic hand-mill, grind! With the money from this salt I'll buy myself a big house."

And the hand-mill went on grinding, until salt was pouring over the sides of the boat. And still the thief sang, "Grind, magic hand-mill, grind! With the money from this salt…"

Suddenly the boat began to tilt. Before the thief could remember to say, "Stop, magic hand-mill, stop!" he was tipped into the water.

The boat sank to the bottom. It settled on the sea-bed with the hand-mill still grinding out salt. The only person who could stop it was the thief. But he was far away, swimming for the shore.

So the magic hand-mill is still down there today, grinding out salt.

And that is why the sea is salty.

The Goblins' Magic Stick

High in the Korean hills lived two brothers, Dogal and Gogal. Their parents were poor, and every day Dogal and Gogal had to go out into the forest to gather firewood. Every day Gogal grumbled and said he didn't want to go, and every day Dogal said, "Come on, Gogal, we must help our parents."

One day Gogal said, "I'm never going to pick up another stick!" and ran off. So Dogal went into the forest alone.

* * *

All day Dogal gathered firewood. Later, he stopped to rest under a big tree. As he was nodding off, something fell into his lap. Dogal opened one eye. It was a ripe walnut.

"I'll give this to Mother," he said, putting the walnut in his pocket.

Another walnut fell into his lap, and then another.

"I'll give this one to Father," he said, "and this one to Gogal."

By then it was growing late, so he set off home.

Now, in the forest there was an old, spooky house. As Dogal was
hurrying past, it grew dark and started to rain.

"Oh dear. I'll have to shelter in the old house," he said.

No sooner was he inside, than he heard a horrible hubbub behind him. Quickly he hid the firewood and climbed up into the rafters. Just in time! A pack of goblins, growling and grunting and waving sticks, ran in from the rain.

The goblins were hungry. They sat down and hammered the floor with their sticks. *Thump! Thump!*

"Come out, food! Come out, drink!" they roared.

Dogal watched. Then he gasped. There on the floor lay a feast of food and drink!

The goblins gobbled and guzzled, then hammered the floor for more. *Thump! Thump!*

"Come out, food! Come out, drink!"

Watching them, Dogal grew hungrier and hungrier. All he had to eat were the walnuts in his pocket. He put one in his mouth and cracked it with his teeth.

CRACK!

The room fell silent.

The goblins jumped to their feet in fright.

"The rafters are cracking! The roof is falling!" they roared, and they ran off into the night.

* * *

Dogal crept down from the rafters. As he went to pick up his firewood, he spotted a goblin stick on the floor.

"They've left behind one of their magic sticks!" he cried. "What a bit of luck!" He picked it up and ran away as fast as he could.

Safe back home, Dogal told his parents all that had happened and showed them what the magic stick could do. His parents were overjoyed. But Gogal, who was watching, grew jealous. He wanted a magic stick of his own.

He found a walnut and hurried to the old, spooky house.

"Scaring goblins is easy," he scoffed, as he hid himself up in the rafters.

* * *

He didn't have to wait long. As soon as it was dark, in ran the goblins, growling and grunting and waving their sticks.

They sat down and hammered on the floor. *Thump! Thump!*

"Come out, gold!" they roared.

Gogal's eyes nearly popped out of his head. Gold coins lay all over the floor.

He couldn't wait. Quickly he cracked his walnut.

CRACK!

The room fell silent. All the goblins looked up.

"It's him again," they growled, "the one who stole our magic stick." They jumped up and pulled Gogal down from the rafters.

"It wasn't me!" cried Gogal.

"He's got a lying tongue," growled the goblins, and they hammered the floor with their sticks. *Thump! Thump!*

"Come out, lying tongue!" they roared.

And Gogal's tongue started to grow longer.

All night the goblins teased Gogal, stretching and shrinking him and pulling his tongue. Then, when daylight came, they chased him away.

When his parents saw him, they asked, "Why is your tongue so long?"

Gogal couldn't answer. But Dogal guessed what had happened.

"Don't worry, Gogal," he said. "I know what to do." He picked up his magic stick and hammered the floor. *Thump! Thump!*

"Go back, tongue!" he cried.

Gogal's tongue shrank back into his mouth and he could speak again.

"Thank you, Dogal, thank you!" he said.

* * *

After that, Gogal never grumbled again. But he would never go near the old, spooky house. And if anyone said 'goblin', Gogal would run off, stuttering, "Gob-gob-gob-goblin!"

A Bit of Shade

It was the hottest day of the year and the sun blazed down from a scorching sky.

A young man was looking for a bit of shade. He came across a zelkova tree with a house nearby. So he sat down in the cool green shade of the zelkova tree.

It wasn't long before
an old man in a tall black
horsehair hat hurried out
of the house.
"Go away!" he shouted.
"This is *my* shade!"
"How can it be your shade?" asked
the young man.
"My great-great-great-grandfather planted
that tree," said the old man, "so its shade belongs to me!"
The young man thought for a moment. "Then will you
sell me your shade?" he asked.
"Sell you the shade of the zelkova tree?" The old man chuckled.
"Yes, I'll sell it to you."
So the young man paid for the shade and sat down again to enjoy it.

As the young man sat in the cool green shade of the zelkova tree, the sun moved slowly across the sky. The young man saw that his bit of shade had grown longer. It now reached the yard of the nearby house. So he went into the yard and sat down there.

It wasn't long before the old man in the tall black horsehair hat hurried out of the house again, shaking his fist.

"Get out!" he shouted. "This is *my* yard!"

"And this is *my* shade," the young man said. "I bought it."

He wouldn't budge, and there was nothing the old man could do about it.

* * *

As the young man sat in the yard in the cool green shade of the zelkova tree, the sun moved further across the sky. The young man saw that his bit of shade had grown even longer. It now reached the porch of the house. So the young man went up to the porch and sat down there.

It wasn't long before the old man in the tall black horsehair hat hurried out again. He was hopping up and down with rage.

"Get out at once!" he shouted. "This is *my* porch."

"And this is *my* shade," said the young man. "I bought it."

He wouldn't budge, and there was nothing the old man could do.

The young man sat enjoying his bit of shade until the sun went down. Then he went home for the night.

The next day he was back, and the day after, and the day after that, sitting in the cool green shade that gradually reached into the yard and then up to the porch of the house.

And people began to laugh at the old man in the tall black horsehair hat, saying, "You sold him that shade. Why don't you buy it back?"

But the young man would not sell back the shade of the zelkova tree.

So in the end the old man crept away, shamefaced, in the middle
of the night, never to be seen again, leaving the young man
his yard, his porch and his house – all for the price of a bit of shade!

Why Pigs have Snouts

Long, long ago, hens had no combs on their heads, dogs had to make do with only three legs, and pigs looked down their long, elegant noses.

One day long, long ago, Hen, Dog and Pig were summoned before the Heavenly Ruler.

As they hurried up to the Heavenly Palace, they started worrying.

"Oh dear," they said. "We must have done something very wrong to be summoned before the Heavenly Ruler!"

But when they reached the palace, they found that they hadn't done anything wrong. Instead, the Heavenly Ruler announced: "I am sending you down to Earth on a mission – to help mankind. Report back to me in a year's time."

Hen, Dog and Pig bowed low and scampered down to Earth.

Hen and Dog both had bright ideas of how to help mankind. But Pig couldn't think of anything.

A year passed, and all three animals were summoned back to the Heavenly Palace.

"Now tell me, how has each of you has helped mankind?" asked the Heavenly Ruler.

Hen stepped forward first, and said, "I helped them eat well, Your Majesty. At the start of each new day. I laid eggs for them."

"You've been a great help, Hen," said the Ruler. "Here is your reward – a beautiful red comb to wear on your head."

Hen bowed. "I will always be grateful for this heavenly gift," she said.

"Now, Dog, tell me how you helped mankind," said the Ruler.

"I guarded men day and night. I kept their houses safe by day while they were out working, and at night they could all sleep soundly," said Dog.

"You, too, have been a great help, Dog," said the Ruler. "Here is your reward – another leg."

Dog bowed. "I am greatly honoured by this heavenly gift," he said, "and I will always keep it clean."

"And now, Pig – how have you helped mankind?" asked the Ruler.

Pig looked down his long, elegant nose, and sniffed.

"Everything I thought of, Hen and Dog were already doing. So there was nothing left for me to do but eat and sleep."

"Pig, you are a disgrace!" exclaimed the Heavenly Ruler. "Off with your nose!"

* * *

And from that day to this,
    hens have had red combs,
        dogs have cocked their hind legs –
            and pigs have had short, snuffly snouts.

The Fierce Old Dried Persimmon

Tiger was hungry.

But everywhere was covered in snow. So one night, he came down from the mountain and padded silently towards a farm. His mouth watered as he made for the cowshed.

That night, a thief was also making his way to the farm, hoping to run off with a cow. As he reached the farm, a cry broke through the silence.

"Just a baby crying," muttered the thief, creeping towards the cowshed.

Tiger also heard the cry. He followed the sound to the house and listened outside the window.

Inside, a mother was singing to her baby.

"Hush-a-bye baby, don't you cry," she sang. "If you do – a tiger will get you!"

"Talk of a tiger – and here I am!" growled Tiger. "How does she know I'm out here?"

The baby went on crying and the mother sang, "Hush-a-bye baby, don't you cry. If you cry... a tiger will come and get you!"

The baby cried even louder.

"That baby should be more afraid of a big tiger like me," Tiger growled.

Again the mother sang, "Hush-a-bye baby, don't you cry..." Then she said, "Look! Here's a dried persimmon."

The baby stopped crying and reached out for the fruit.

Tiger was puzzled. "Only something much fiercer than me could stop that baby crying. What could it be?"

Now, any other tiger would have known that a dried persimmon is a sweet, delicious fruit that babies love to suck. But this tiger didn't know that. He thought there was something fierce out on the prowl. So he fled to the cowshed and hid in the darkest corner.

Meanwhile, the thief was inside the cowshed, feeling around for a cow to steal. Finding something warm and furry in the corner, he tied a rope around its neck.

Tiger leapt up in terror. "That fierce old dried persimmon's got me!" he moaned.

And the thief thought, "This cow's frisky. Perhaps it would be quicker to ride her out of here."

He jumped up on Tiger's back. Tiger gasped, and shot out of the cowshed.

"This cow runs fast," thought the thief, and hung on tightly to its ears.

When Tiger felt his ears pulled, he roared.

And the thief thought, "This cow doesn't sound like any cow I've ever heard. It sounds more like... a TIGER!" He groaned. "How could I mistake a tiger for a cow?"

At that moment, Tiger dived into a forest and the thief saw his chance. He grabbed a low-hanging branch and swung off its back. Tiger ran on, while the thief looked for a hole to hide in.

* * *

When Tiger was sure nothing was chasing him, he collapsed in the snow, roaring with relief.

A rabbit poked out his head to see what had happened.

"There's something horrible on the prowl tonight," said Tiger. And he told Rabbit all about the dried persimmon.

Rabbit smiled and said, "Old dried persimmons don't frighten me."

"This one's very fierce," said Tiger.

"I'd like to see it," said Rabbit. So, with Tiger following, Rabbit set off to find the fierce old dried persimmon. But of course he didn't find it. All he found was a frightened thief hiding in a hole.

"Why are you so frightened?" Rabbit asked the thief.

"There's a big, fierce tiger on the prowl," replied the thief, and told Rabbit all about it.

Rabbit chuckled. "Big, fierce tigers don't frighten me," he said. "Just watch." And he called Tiger over.

"I've found what you were telling me about," Rabbit said. "It's in this hole." Then he stood close to the thief's hole and said loudly, "See, I'm not afraid of anything!"

The thief saw Tiger – and was so scared that he pulled Rabbit in by his tail to block the entrance.

Rabbit squealed, and Tiger said, "Silly rabbit – now the fierce old dried persimmon's got you!"

Rabbit tried to wriggle free, but the thief tied a piece of string to his tail and pulled him in even harder.

"I told you that persimmon was dangerous," said Tiger. "Now it's going to eat you!"

Rabbit squealed and wriggled and pulled so hard, his tail came off. Tiger watched in horror, then fled back up the mountain.

And ever since then, rabbits have had small fluffy tufts for tails.

Me First!

In the days when tigers smoked long pipes and animals could speak,
Deer, Hare and Toad held a party. They put the food on small tables,
ready to serve the oldest animal first.

But who was the oldest – Deer, Hare or Toad?

"Me," said Deer. "I'm the oldest. I should be served first."

"No, it's me," said Hare. "I'm the oldest."

And so they went on, until Toad said, "You must both say why you
think you're the oldest."

"I'm the oldest," said Deer, "because when the world was made,
I climbed up a ladder with a hammer and nails and pinned the first stars
to the sky. So I should be served first."

"You're a very old deer," said Hare. "But I'm older still, because when
the world was made, I planted the tree that grew the wood that was made
into the ladder you climbed up, when you pinned the first stars to the sky.
So I should be served first."

Toad listened to Deer and Hare, and then said sadly, "All this talk of long ago reminds me that I once had three sons.

When the world was made, my sons all planted trees.

My third son planted the tree that grew the wood that was made into the handle of the hammer Deer used, when he pinned the first stars to the sky.

And before that, my second son planted the tree that grew the wood that was made into the plough that dug the furrow for the silvery river of the Milky Way.

"And before that, my first son planted the tree that grew the wood that was made into the frame that carried the sun and the moon to their places up in the sky."

Toad wiped his eyes. "My three sons died long ago, and you, Deer and Hare, have just reminded me of them."

Deer and Hare looked at one another. It was clear that Toad was the oldest of the three. And they had to agree that he was a very old toad indeed!

So Toad was served first. Once that was done, the party began – and a good time was had by all!

The Land of the Dragon King

Shim Chong lived with her father by the sea.
Her mother had died and her father, who was
blind and unable to work, was forced to take his
little daughter out begging.

When she grew older, Shim Chong worked as a maid.
Each day she left home early in the morning and came back at dusk.

One day, she was late coming home. Her father set off to meet her,
but as he followed the dark path along the river-bank, he stumbled and
fell into the water. He would have drowned, but a monk heard his cries
and pulled him out.

Seeing that the old man was blind, the monk said, "Your sight can
be restored – but only if you send three hundred sacks of rice to the
temple as an offering to Buddha."

"Three hundred sacks of rice!" exclaimed the old man. "I don't
even have three bowls of rice!"

"It must be three hundred," said the monk. So Shim Chong's father promised to deliver the rice to the temple.

When he reached home, his daughter was back and he told her what had happened. "How," he asked, "can I pay for three hundred sacks of rice?" Shim Chong prayed that they would find a way.

* * *

A few days later, a merchant ship carrying a cargo of rice anchored in the harbour. The ship had been driven off-course by the terrible power of the Dragon King, who lived beneath the East Sea. Now the ship's crew were looking for a girl to sacrifice to the Dragon King so that he would grant them a safe passage to China.

When Shim Chong learnt that they would pay the girl handsomely, she ran to the sailors and offered herself.

"You will have to jump overboard into the sea," the sailors told her.

Shim Chong nodded.

"Then name your price."

"Three hundred sacks of rice," said Shim Chong.

The sailors agreed. "We will come for you in three days," they said. "We sail with the tide, at full moon."

But even after the sacks of rice had been delivered to the temple, still Shim Chong's father could not see. And when Shim Chong told him that she had sold herself as a sacrifice to the Dragon King, he wept.

"Now I am blind *and* I have lost my beautiful daughter!"

The seas were calm when the merchant ship set sail with Shim Chong on board. Then a storm struck. The wind roared. The seas swelled. Waves crashed over the boat.

"The Dragon King is angry!" cried the sailors. "We must sacrifice the girl to calm him!"

They led Shim Chong to the edge of the boat. She stood for a moment, staring at the wild seas. Then she closed her eyes, said a prayer for her father and jumped overboard.

Instantly the storm died down and the seas grew calm. The sailors stared sadly at the place where Shim Chong had disappeared. Then they sailed on their way.

***

Beneath the sea, a shoal of fish swept Shim Chong up, carried her down to the land of the Dragon King and laid her at his feet.

The Dragon King stood looking down at Shim Chong.

"I will make this beautiful girl a princess," he said.

And when Shim Chong opened her eyes, she saw the Dragon King's palace and heard around her the music and laughter of his underwater kingdom. The King's family dressed her in fine clothes and welcomed her into their midst.

But Shim Chong was not happy. Every day she thought of her father, knowing he would become a beggar again without her to support him.

Seeing how much Shim Chong loved her father, the Dragon King knew she would never be happy underwater. So he freed her, floating her back up to the world of men inside a large lotus flower.

Some fishermen spotted the lotus flower bobbing on the waves. They plucked it from the water and presented it to their ruler. As the King gazed in wonder at the strange flower, its petals began to unfurl and out stepped Shim Chong.

The moment he saw her, the King fell in love with her and plans were made for their marriage. Shim Chong was happy – but still she longed to see her father. One day, she asked the King if he would invite all the blind people in his kingdom to their wedding feast. The King was puzzled by her strange request, but he agreed, and sent out a proclamation.

For days, blind men and women flocked to the palace from all around. Every day Shim Chong searched among them for her father, but could not find him.

Then, on the very last day of the feast, Shim Chong saw a familiar figure shuffle through the palace gates. All heads turned as the Queen ran and threw her arms around the ragged old beggar.

"Father!" she cried.

"Is that my daughter's voice?" asked the beggar. "I thought she was dead!" Astonished, he opened his eyes wide – and found that he could see!

And what was the first thing he saw? His beautiful daughter, Shim Chong.

The King warmly welcomed his new father-in-law, and everyone rejoiced that Shim Chong's devotion had finally been rewarded.

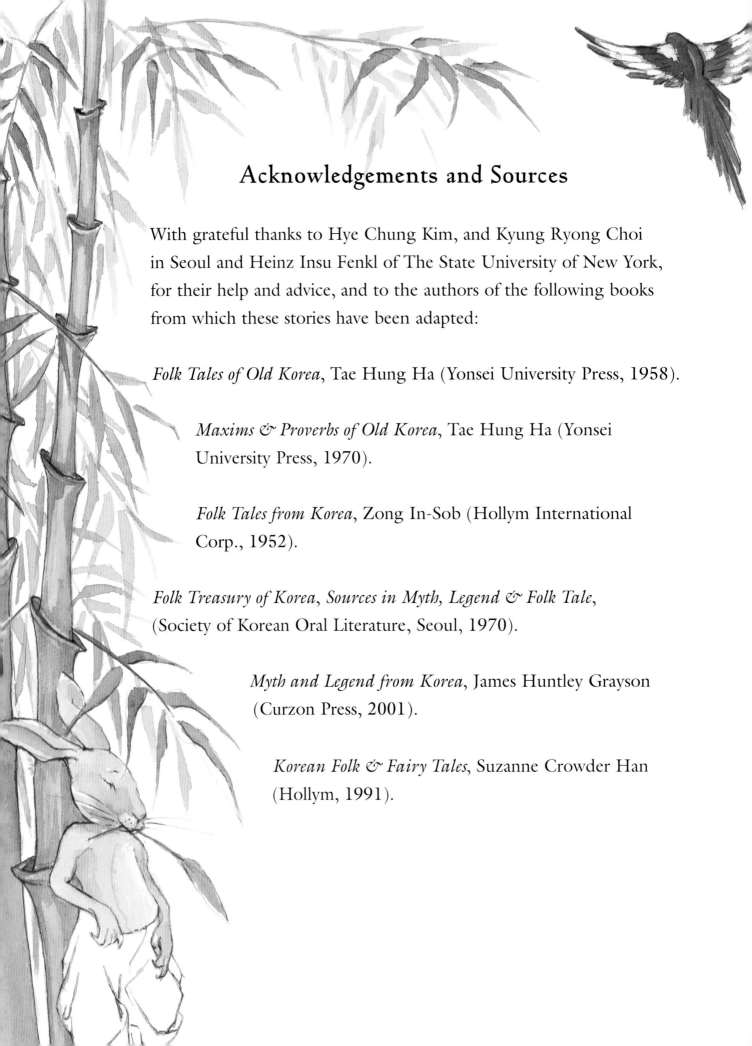

Acknowledgements and Sources

With grateful thanks to Hye Chung Kim, and Kyung Ryong Choi in Seoul and Heinz Insu Fenkl of The State University of New York, for their help and advice, and to the authors of the following books from which these stories have been adapted:

Folk Tales of Old Korea, Tae Hung Ha (Yonsei University Press, 1958).

Maxims & Proverbs of Old Korea, Tae Hung Ha (Yonsei University Press, 1970).

Folk Tales from Korea, Zong In-Sob (Hollym International Corp., 1952).

Folk Treasury of Korea, Sources in Myth, Legend & Folk Tale, (Society of Korean Oral Literature, Seoul, 1970).

Myth and Legend from Korea, James Huntley Grayson (Curzon Press, 2001).

Korean Folk & Fairy Tales, Suzanne Crowder Han (Hollym, 1991).